A Note to Parents and Caregivers:

Read-it! Readers are for children who are just starting on the amazing road to reading. These beautiful books support both the acquisition of reading skills and the love of books.

 The PURPLE LEVEL presents basic topics and objects using high frequency words and simple language patterns.

 The RED LEVEL presents familiar topics using common words and repeating sentence patterns.

 The BLUE LEVEL presents new ideas using a larger vocabulary and varied sentence structure.

 The YELLOW LEVEL presents more challenging ideas, a broad vocabulary, and wide variety in sentence structure.

 The GREEN LEVEL presents more complex ideas, an extended vocabulary range, and expanded language structures.

 The ORANGE LEVEL presents a wide range of ideas and concepts using challenging vocabulary and complex language structures.

When sharing a book with your child, read in short stretches, pausing often to talk about the pictures. Have your child turn the pages and point to the pictures and familiar words. And be sure to reread favorite stories or parts of stories.

There is no right or wrong way to share books with children. Find time to read with your child, and pass on the legacy of literacy.

Adria F. Klein, Ph.D.
Professor Emeritus
California State University
San Bernardino, California

Editor: Nick Healy
Designer: Tracy Kaehler
Page Production: Lori Bye
Creative Director: Keith Griffin
Editorial Director: Carol Jones
The illustrations in this book were created in acrylics.

Picture Window Books
5115 Excelsior Boulevard
Suite 232
Minneapolis, MN 55416
877-845-8392
www.picturewindowbooks.com

Printed in the United States of America.

Library of Congress Cataloging-in-Publication Data
Dougherty, Terri.
Emily's pictures / by Terri Dougherty ; illustrated by Ronnie Rooney.
p. cm. — (Read-it! readers)
Summary: Emily would like to be able to draw, but her trees look like mashed
potatoes and her houses like ketchup bottles until she tries something different.
ISBN-13: 978-1-4048-2409-6 (hardcover)
ISBN-10: 1-4048-2409-X (hardcover)
[1. Drawing—Fiction. 2. Left- and right-handedness—Fiction. 3. African
Americans—Fiction.] I. Rooney, Ronnie, ill. II. Title. III. Series.
PZ7.D74436Emi 2006
[E]—dc22   2006003434

Emily's Pictures

by Terri Dougherty
illustrated by Ronnie Rooney

Special thanks to our advisers for their expertise:

Adria F. Klein, Ph.D.
Professor Emeritus, California State University
San Bernardino, California

Susan Kesselring, M.A.
Literacy Educator
Rosemount–Apple Valley–Eagan (Minnesota) School District

PICTURE WINDOW BOOKS
Minneapolis, Minnesota

Emily wished she could draw well.
She wished she could draw circles.

She wished she could draw pretty faces, trees, and houses.

Emily tried and tried. But she
did not like her drawings.

"I can't draw anything right," she said. "All of my pictures are a mess."

Emily could not draw circles. They looked like eggs.

She could not draw trees. They looked like mashed potatoes sitting on a stick.

The houses she drew looked even worse. They were all too skinny. They looked like bottles of ketchup.

Emily did not know what to do. She did not want to give up.

But her pictures were not turning out right.

"Try using a new pencil, Emily,"
said her mother.

Emily tried a sharp new pencil. Her circles still looked like eggs.

"Try using a different kind of paper," said her father.

Emily took a piece of green paper.
Now her trees looked like green
mashed potatoes.

Emily scribbled over her trees. She dropped her pencil.

She was ready to give up. "I cannot get it right," she said.

Then she grabbed the pencil with her left hand. She drew a frowning face near her messy trees.

The face was neat and round.
"Wait a minute," she said. "I can
do it!"

"I don't have to give up drawing," Emily said. "I just have to draw with my left hand."

Then she took a clean sheet
of paper and drew a kitten.
Her picture was perfect.

More *Read-it!* Readers

Bright pictures and fun stories help you practice your reading skills. Look for more books at your level.

Looking for a specific title or level? A complete list of *Read-it!* Readers is available on our Web site:
www.picturewindowbooks.com